## Dear Parent:
## Your child's love of rea

Every child learns to read in a differ            n
speed. Some go back and forth between reading levels and read
favourite books again and again. Others read through each level in
order. You can help your young reader improve and become more
confident by encouraging his or her own interests and abilities. From
books your child reads with you to the first books he or she reads
alone, there are I Can Read Books for every stage of reading:

### SHARED READING
Basic language, word repetition, and whimsical illustrations,
ideal for sharing with your emergent reader

### BEGINNING READING
Short sentences, familiar words, and simple concepts
for children eager to read on their own

### READING WITH HELP
Engaging stories, longer sentences, and language play
for developing readers

### READING ALONE
Complex plots, challenging vocabulary, and high-interest topics
for the independent reader

### ADVANCED READING
Short paragraphs, chapters, and exciting themes
for the perfect bridge to chapter books

**I Can Read Books** have introduced children to the joy of reading
since 1957. Featuring award-winning authors and illustrators and a
fabulous cast of beloved characters, I Can Read Books set the
standard for beginning readers.

A lifetime of discovery begins with the magical words **"I Can Read!"**

*Visit www.icanread.com for information*
*on enriching your child's reading experience.*

# Meet the Masters

Kung Fu Panda™ & © 2008 DreamWorks Animation L.L.C.

First published in the UK by HarperCollins Children's Books in 2008

1 3 5 7 9 10 8 6 4 2

ISBN-10: 0-00-726929-3

ISBN-13: 978-0-00-726929-7

A CIP catalogue record for this title is available from the British Library.

www.harpercollinschildrensbooks.co.uk

Book design by Rick Farley

Printed and bound in China

# I Can Read!

READING WITH HELP 2

DREAMWORKS

# KUNG FU PANDA

## Meet the Masters

Adapted by Catherine Hapka

Pencils by Charles Grosvenor

Colour by Lydia Halverson

HarperCollins *Children's Books*

Everyone in the Valley of Peace
knew the legend
of the Dragon Warrior.

It was said that this great hero
would save the valley
in its darkest hour.

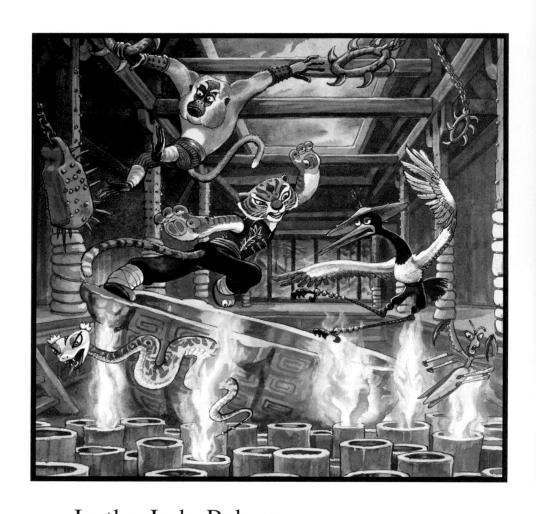

In the Jade Palace,

Master Shifu

watched the Furious Five practice.

The Five were the best

kung fu warriors in the kingdom.

Shifu was a tough master.

"Do not fear pain," he said sternly.

"As long as you feel it,

you know you're still alive."

Master Oogway was

the wisest creature in all of China.

He knew it was time

to choose the Dragon Warrior.

"I had a vision," he told Shifu.

"The valley is in danger.

Tai Lung is returning."

Tai Lung was once

Shifu's best pupil.

He had talent

and was destined for greatness.

He wanted to be the Dragon Warrior.

But Tai Lung was not chosen.

That made him very angry.

Shifu had to banish him to prison.

Who would Oogway choose

to fight Tai Lung now?

Tigress was loyal, brave, and strong.
Her powerful kung fu style
brought fear to her enemies.

Tigress feared nothing and no one.

She wanted to fight Tai Lung

and protect the valley.

Crane knew that sometimes

talking was better than fighting.

But Crane was a kung fu master, too.

His fighting style looked like dancing.

Crane was so quick and nimble

that he could wear out his enemies.

Crane was ready

to be the Dragon Warrior

if he was chosen.

Monkey was the joker of the group.

He was playful and acrobatic.

But he was deadly serious

when an enemy was near!

He looked forward to playing

with Tai Lung

before finishing him off.

The Furious Five could always rely
on Viper in times of trouble.
Viper was a skillful warrior
with a deadly strike.

20

Viper moved as fast as lightning.
She knew that this would make her
a great Dragon Warrior.

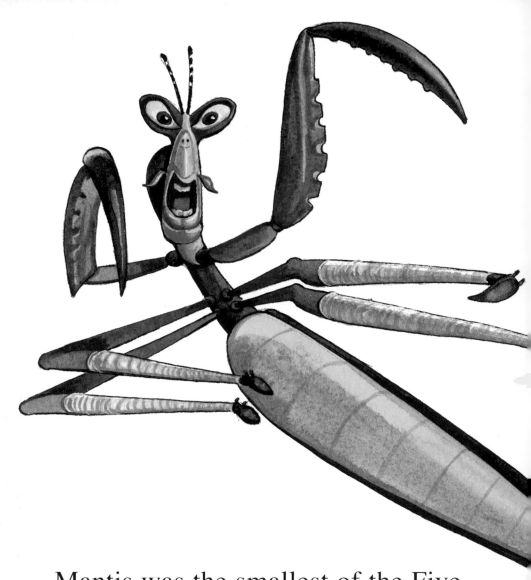

Mantis was the smallest of the Five.

But his skills were mighty indeed.

He had incredible speed

and was nearly invisible in a fight.

He planned to defeat Tai Lung

with a fast jab

from his sharp front legs.

A panda named Po

had heard many tales

of the Dragon Warrior.

Po loved kung fu

and dreamed of great battles.

But he was big and clumsy.

He wasn't anything like

a kung fu master.

Mr. Ping was Po's dad.

He owned a noodle shop.

He didn't care about kung fu.

He only cared about noodles.

Po's dad was sure that one day
his son would give up
his silly kung fu dreams
and learn to love noodles.

In a faraway prison,
Commander Vachir guarded
only one prisoner, Tai Lung.
Shifu sent Zeng the goose
to warn the commander
that Tai Lung would soon escape.

Zeng was nervous
being so close to Tai Lung.
He was even more nervous
when Tai Lung escaped
and grabbed him by the neck!

29

Tai Lung headed for the valley.

It was time to choose

the Dragon Warrior.

Would it be Tigress, Crane,

Monkey, Viper, or Mantis?

Oogway was getting ready to decide
when Po crash-landed in front of him.
"How interesting," Oogway said.
"The universe has brought us
the Dragon Warrior!"

Could Po fulfill his destiny
as the Dragon Warrior?
Oogway believed in him.
All that was needed now
was for Po to believe in himself!